BBC

DOCTOR WHO

POLICE PUBLIC BOX

2014

DIARY

MALLON
Melbourne

BBC

DOCTOR WHO

2014

DIARY

2014

JANUARY

M	T	W	T	F	S	S
		1	2	3	4	5
6	7	8	9	10	11	12
13	14	15	16	17	18	19
20	21	22	23	24	25	26
27	28	29	30	31		

FEBRUARY

M	T	W	T	F	S	S
					1	2
3	4	5	6	7	8	9
10	11	12	13	14	15	16
17	18	19	20	21	22	23
24	25	26	27	28		

MARCH

M	T	W	T	F	S	S
31					1	2
3	4	5	6	7	8	9
10	11	12	13	14	15	16
17	18	19	20	21	22	23
24	25	26	27	28	29	30

APRIL

M	T	W	T	F	S	S
	1	2	3	4	5	6
7	8	9	10	11	12	13
14	15	16	17	18	19	20
21	22	23	24	25	26	27
28	29	30				

MAY

M	T	W	T	F	S	S
			1	2	3	4
5	6	7	8	9	10	11
12	13	14	15	16	17	18
19	20	21	22	23	24	25
26	27	28	29	30	31	

JUNE

M	T	W	T	F	S	S
30						1
2	3	4	5	6	7	8
9	10	11	12	13	14	15
16	17	18	19	20	21	22
23	24	25	26	27	28	29

JULY

M	T	W	T	F	S	S
	1	2	3	4	5	6
7	8	9	10	11	12	13
14	15	16	17	18	19	20
21	22	23	24	25	26	27
28	29	30	31			

AUGUST

M	T	W	T	F	S	S
				1	2	3
4	5	6	7	8	9	10
11	12	13	14	15	16	17
18	19	20	21	22	23	24
25	26	27	28	29	30	31

SEPTEMBER

M	T	W	T	F	S	S
1	2	3	4	5	6	7
8	9	10	11	12	13	14
15	16	17	18	19	20	21
22	23	24	25	26	27	28
29	30					

OCTOBER

M	T	W	T	F	S	S
		1	2	3	4	5
6	7	8	9	10	11	12
13	14	15	16	17	18	19
20	21	22	23	24	25	26
27	28	29	30	31		

NOVEMBER

M	T	W	T	F	S	S
					1	2
3	4	5	6	7	8	9
10	11	12	13	14	15	16
17	18	19	20	21	22	23
24	25	26	27	28	29	30

DECEMBER

M	T	W	T	F	S	S
1	2	3	4	5	6	7
8	9	10	11	12	13	14
15	16	17	18	19	20	21
22	23	24	25	26	27	28
29	30	31				

2015

JANUARY

M	T	W	T	F	S	S
			1	2	3	4
5	6	7	8	9	10	11
12	13	14	15	16	17	18
19	20	21	22	23	24	25
26	27	28	29	30	31	

FEBRUARY

M	T	W	T	F	S	S
						1
2	3	4	5	6	7	8
9	10	11	12	13	14	15
16	17	18	19	20	21	22
23	24	25	26	27	28	

MARCH

M	T	W	T	F	S	S
30	31					1
2	3	4	5	6	7	8
9	10	11	12	13	14	15
16	17	18	19	20	21	22
23	24	25	26	27	28	29

APRIL

M	T	W	T	F	S	S
	1	2	3	4	5	
6	7	8	9	10	11	12
13	14	15	16	17	18	19
20	21	22	23	24	25	26
27	28	29	30			

MAY

M	T	W	T	F	S	S
				1	2	3
4	5	6	7	8	9	10
11	12	13	14	15	16	17
18	19	20	21	22	23	24
25	26	27	28	29	30	31

JUNE

M	T	W	T	F	S	S
1	2	3	4	5	6	7
8	9	10	11	12	13	14
15	16	17	18	19	20	21
22	23	24	25	26	27	28
29	30					

JULY

M	T	W	T	F	S	S
	1	2	3	4	5	
6	7	8	9	10	11	12
13	14	15	16	17	18	19
20	21	22	23	24	25	26
27	28	29	30	31		

AUGUST

M	T	W	T	F	S	S
31					1	2
3	4	5	6	7	8	9
10	11	12	13	14	15	16
17	18	19	20	21	22	23
24	25	26	27	28	29	30

SEPTEMBER

M	T	W	T	F	S	S
	1	2	3	4	5	6
7	8	9	10	11	12	13
14	15	16	17	18	19	20
21	22	23	24	25	26	27
28	29	30				

OCTOBER

M	T	W	T	F	S	S
			1	2	3	4
5	6	7	8	9	10	11
12	13	14	15	16	17	18
19	20	21	22	23	24	25
26	27	28	29	30	31	

NOVEMBER

M	T	W	T	F	S	S
30						1
2	3	4	5	6	7	8
9	10	11	12	13	14	15
16	17	18	19	20	21	22
23	24	25	26	27	28	29

DECEMBER

M	T	W	T	F	S	S
	1	2	3	4	5	6
7	8	9	10	11	12	13
14	15	16	17	18	19	20
21	22	23	24	25	26	27
28	29	30	31			

PUBLISHER'S NOTE

This year's Doctor Who diary covers Series 7 in its entirety, beginning with Asylum of the Daleks, in which the Doctor is kidnapped and taken to the Dalek Parliament, and ending with the nail-biting series finale, The Name of the Doctor, in which the Doctor follows his kidnapped friends to the planet of Trenzalore – the one place the Doctor should never go! Over the course of the series we say good-bye to Amy Pond and her husband Rory, who fall victim to the terrifying powers of the Weeping Angels, and his heartbreak leads the Doctor to travel alone for some time. That is until he stumbles upon Clara. Together they have battled monsters in the wi-fi in modern-day London, tackled Old Gods on distant alien planets, found themselves trapped in a Russian submarine with a deadly Ice Warrior passenger, investigated the Witch of the Well at Caliburn House, delved into the heart of the TARDIS whilst pursued by Time Zombies, faced the Crimson Horror in Victorian Yorkshire and come face to face with an army of upgraded Cybermen at Hedgewick's World of Wonders in the far future. In seeking to unravel the mystery surrounding Clara, the 'Impossible Girl', the Doctor's own greatest secret has now been revealed…

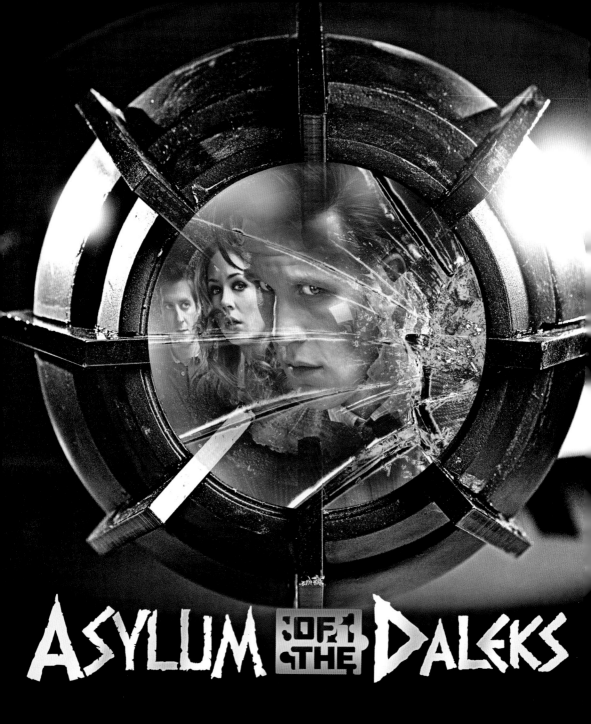

ASYLUM 1 OF 1 THE DALEKS

Kidnapped by his oldest foe, the Doctor is
forced on an impossible mission – to a place
even the Daleks are too terrified to enter ...
There he befriends a fiesty young woman who
has hacked into the planet's computer systems.
Can she save the Doctor and herself?

M T W T F S S M T W T F S S M T W T F S S
      1 2 3 4 5 6 7 8 9 10 11 12 13 14 15 16 17 18 19
20 21 22 23 24 25 26 27 28 29 30 31

JANUARY

30 **Monday**

31 **Tuesday**

1 **Wednesday**

New Year's Day

JANUARY

2 **Thursday**

3 **Friday**

4 **Saturday**

5 **Sunday**

ASYLUM OF THE DALEKS

Amy and Rory on
their way up to the
Dalek Parliament

6 Monday

7 Tuesday

8 Wednesday

9 Thursday

10 Friday

11 Saturday

12 Sunday

M	T	W	T	F	S	S	M	T	W	T	F	S	S	M	T	W	T	F	S	S
		1	2	3	4	5	6	7	8	9	10	11	12	13	14	15	16	17	18	19
20	21	22	23	24	25	26	27	28	29	30	31									

JANUARY

Oswin Oswald has been trapped on
the Dalek planet since her starship
crashed there a year ago

A Dalek's view of
the Doctor

ASYLUM OF THE DALEKS

13 Monday

14 Tuesday

15 Wednesday

16 Thursday

17 Friday

18 Saturday

19 Sunday

The Dalek Parliament

M	T	W	T	F	S	S	M	T	W	T	F	S	S
1	2	3	4	5	6	7	8	9	10	11	12	13	14	15	16	17	18	19
20	21	22	23	24	25	26	27	28	29	30	31

Darla, a humanoid Dalek
puppet, who lures the Doctor
to the Daleks' home world of
Skaro and then teleports him
to the Parliament of the Daleks

DINOSAURS
ON A SPACESHIP

The Doctor battles to save an unmanned spaceship and its impossible cargo ... of dinosaurs! Accompanied by Queen Nefertiti and a big game hunter he must try to get it back on course before it crashes into Earth.

JANUARY

M	T	W	T	F	S	S	M	T	W	T	F	S	S	M	T	W	T	F	S	S
		1	2	3	4	5	6	7	8	9	10	11	12	13	14	15	16	17	18	19
20	21	22	23	24	25	26	27	28	29	30	31									

20 Monday

Martin Luther King Day

21 Tuesday

22 Wednesday

23 Thursday

24 Friday

25 Saturday

26 Sunday

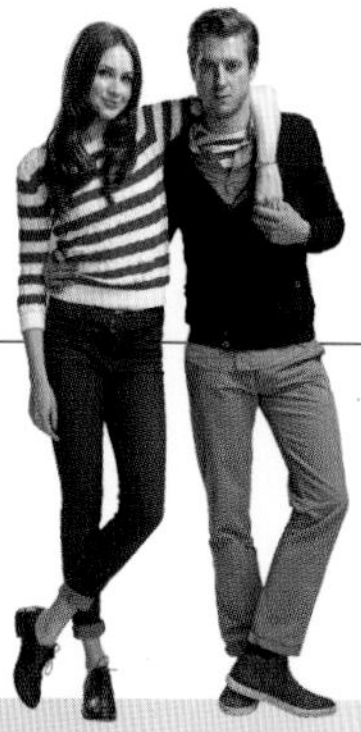

DINOSAURS ON A SPACESHIP

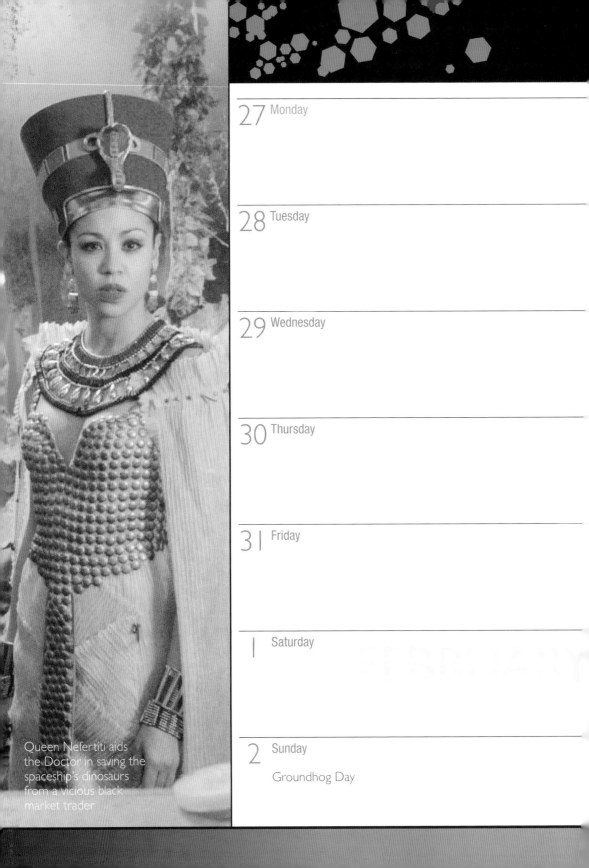

Queen Nefertiti aids the Doctor in saving the spaceship's dinosaurs from a vicious black market trader

27 Monday

28 Tuesday

29 Wednesday

30 Thursday

31 Friday

1 Saturday

2 Sunday

Groundhog Day

M	T	W	T	F	S	S	M	T	W	T	F	S	S	M	T	W	T	F	S	S
		1	2	3	4	5	6	7	8	9	10	11	12	13	14	15	16	17	18	19
20	21	22	23	24	25	26	27	28	29	30	31									

JANUARY

The Doctor catches a ride on the back
of one of the dinosaurs – a Triceratops

DINOSAURS ON A SPACESHIP

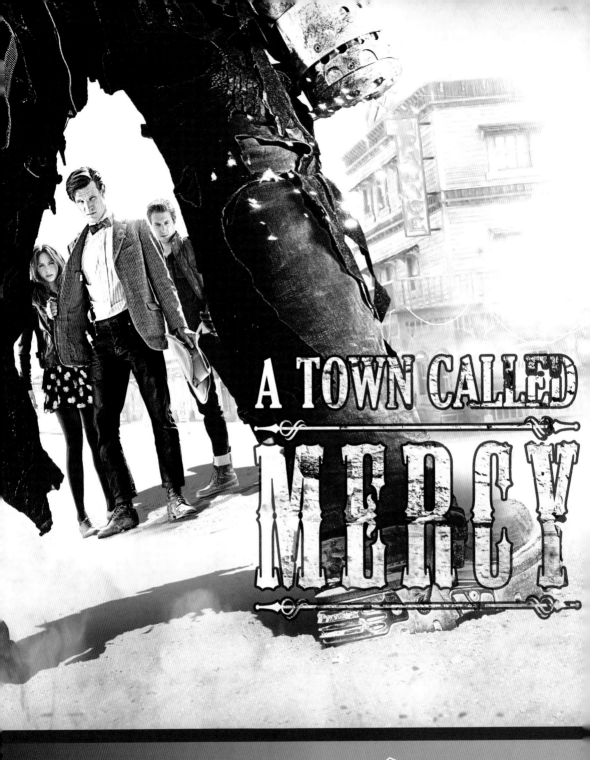

A TOWN CALLED MERCY

The Doctor gets a Stetson (and a gun!) and finds himself a reluctant marshall in the small, dusty western American town of Mercy during the days of gunslingers; although in this instance the Gunslinger is a cyborg.

FEBRUARY

3 Monday

4 Tuesday

5 Wednesday

6 Thursday

7 Friday

8 Saturday

9 Sunday

Rory and Amy in
the Sheriff's office

A TOWN CALLED MERCY

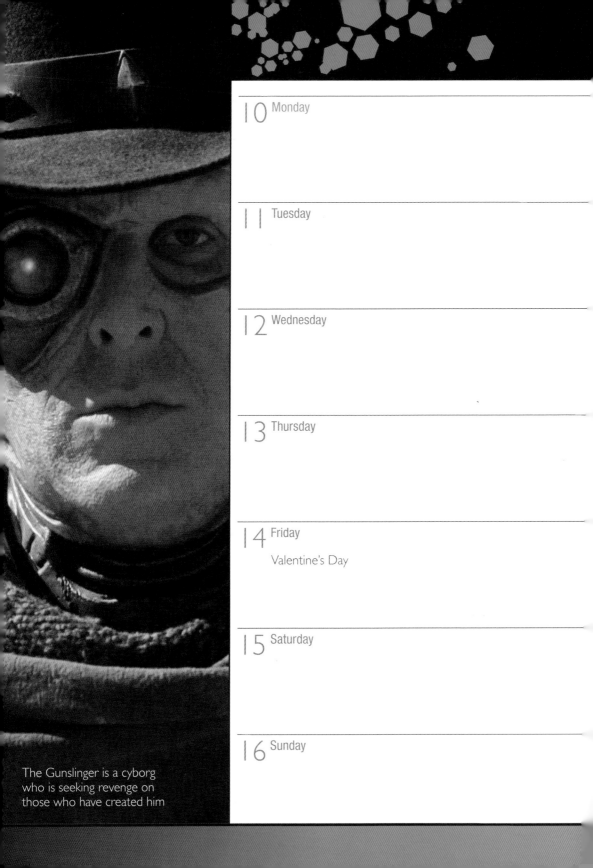

10 Monday

11 Tuesday

12 Wednesday

13 Thursday

14 Friday

Valentine's Day

15 Saturday

16 Sunday

The Gunslinger is a cyborg
who is seeking revenge on
those who have created him

FEBRUARY

			S	M	T	W	T	F	S	S	M	T	W	T	F	S	S
					1	2	3	4	5	6	7	8	9	10	11	12	13	14	15	16
17	18	19	20	21	22	23	24	25	26	27	28

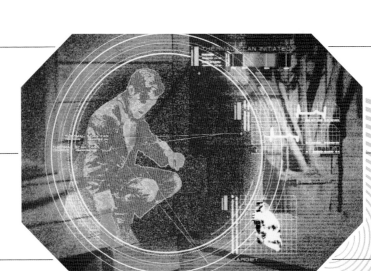

Despite hiding behind a
wall, the Doctor is still
visible to the Gunslinger

Kahler-Jex, an alien who crashed near Mercy and has been living there for the last 10 years

| 17 | Monday |
| | Presidents Day |

| 18 | Tuesday |

| 19 | Wednesday |

| 20 | Thursday |

| 21 | Friday |

| 22 | Saturday |

| 23 | Sunday |

		S	M	T	W	T	F	S	S	M	T	W		F	S	S
						1	2	3	4	5	6	7	8	9	10	11	12	13	14	15	16
17	18	19	20	21	22	23	24	25	26	27	28					

FEBRUARY

The Doctor, about to ride off to retrieve
the TARDIS so he can evacuate the town

High noon
in Mercy

A TOWN CALLED MERCY

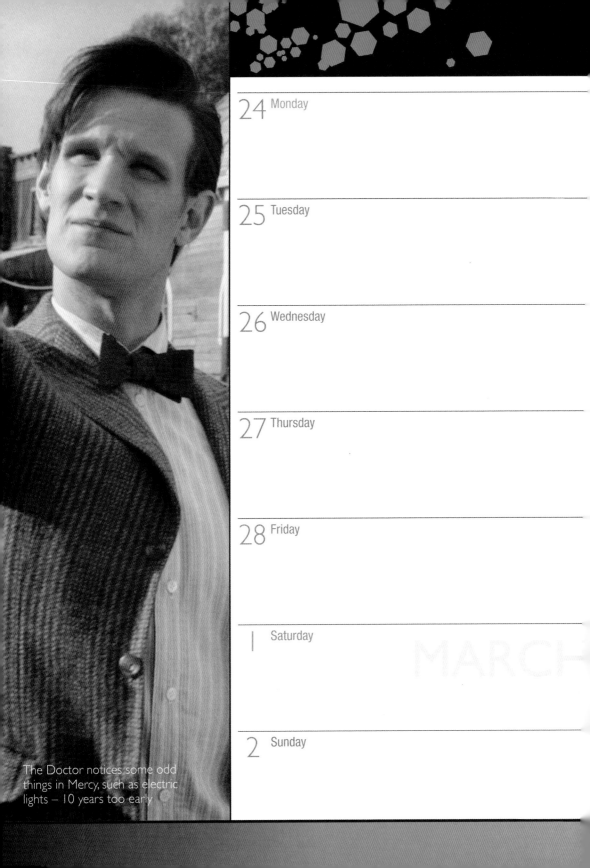

24 Monday

25 Tuesday

26 Wednesday

27 Thursday

28 Friday

1 Saturday

MARCH

2 Sunday

The Doctor notices some odd things in Mercy, such as electric lights – 10 years too early

			M	T	W	T	F	S	S	S	M	T			F	S	S
					1	2	3	4	5	6	7	8	9	10	11	12	13	14	15	16
17	18	19	20	21	22	23	24	25	26	27	28						

FEBRUARY

The Doctor looks over Kahler-Jex's alien
spacecraft beyond the outskirts of town

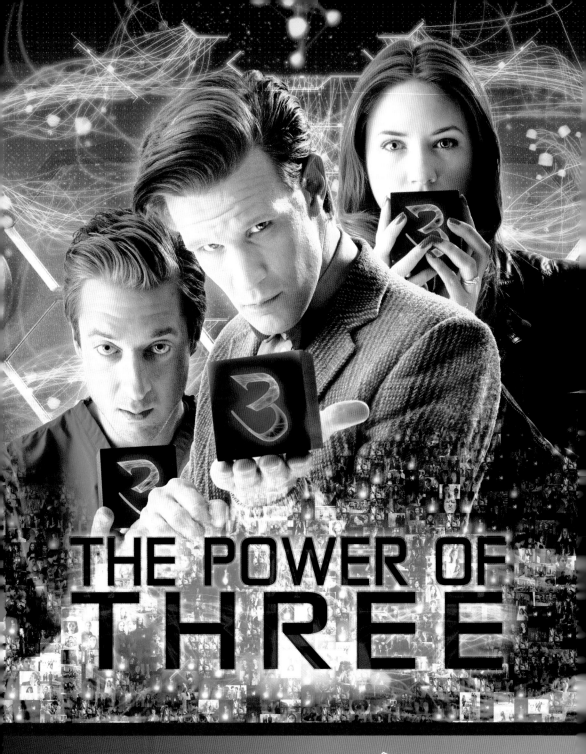

THE POWER OF
THREE

The Doctor and the Ponds puzzle over an
unlikely invader of Earth, millions of small,
identical black boxes that appear all over the
planet at the same time. Just exactly why are
they here and what will they do?

M	T	W	T	F	S	S	M	T	W	T	F	S	S	M	T	W	T	F	S	S
					1	2	3	4	5	6	7	8	9	10	11	12	13	14	15	16
17	18	19	20	21	22	23	24	25	26	27	28	29	30	31						

MARCH

3 Monday

4 Tuesday

5 Wednesday

6 Thursday

7 Friday

8 Saturday

9 Sunday

Daylight Saving (start)

THE POWER OF THREE

10 Monday

11 Tuesday

12 Wednesday

13 Thursday

14 Friday

15 Saturday

16 Sunday

Kate Stewart, the head of scientific research at UNIT and daughter of the Doctor's friend and former UNIT commander, Brigadier Lethbridge-Stewart

MARCH

M	T	W	T	F	S	S	M	T	W	T	F	S	S
				1	2	3	4	5	6	7	8	9	10	11	12	13	14	15	16
17	18	19	20	21	22	23	24	25	26	27	28	29	30	31

Amy and the Doctor contemplate one
of the millions of small black boxes that
mysteriously appear all around the world

Rory's father, Brian, lends a hand at the hospital, before being captured by monstrous orderlies

17 Monday

St Patrick's Day

18 Tuesday

19 Wednesday

20 Thursday

21 Friday

22 Saturday

23 Sunday

			S	M	T	W	T	F	S	S	M	T	W	T	F	S	S
			1	2	3	4	5	6	7	8	9	10	11	12	13	14	15	16
17	18	19	20	21	22	23	24	25	26	27	28	29	30	31

MARCH

The Doctor examines a young girl in the hospital's waiting room, who turns out to be an android

The Doctor and Amy find Rory and others unconscious on an alien spaceship

THE POWER OF THREE

24 Monday

25 Tuesday

26 Wednesday

27 Thursday

28 Friday

29 Saturday

30 Sunday

The Doctor encounters a hologram of a Shakri, self-appointed pest controllers of the universe

S	S	M	T	W	T	F	S	S	M	T	W	T	F	S	S
			1	2	3	4	5	6	7	8	9	10	11	12	13	14	15	16
17	18	19	20	21	22	23	24	25	26	27	28	29	30	31

MARCH

Two hospital orderlies with distorted mouths

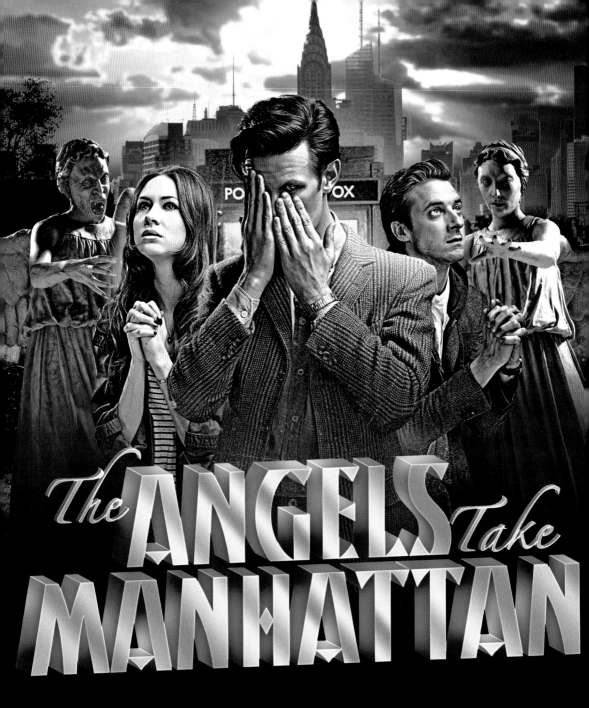

The ANGELS Take MANHATTAN

Weeping Angels are using 1930s Manhattan as a breeding ground, creating huge time distortions. The Doctor and Amy race against the events depicted in a detective novel as they attempt to find and rescue Rory from their evil clutches.

M T W T F S S M T W T F S S M T W T F S S
1 2 3 4 5 6 7 8 9 10 11 12 13 14 15 16 17 18 19 20
21 22 23 24 25 26 27 28 29 30

APRIL

31 | Monday

1 | Tuesday

April Fool's Day   APRIL

2 | Wednesday

3 | Thursday

4 | Friday

5 | Saturday

6 | Sunday

THE ANGELS TAKE MANHATTAN

7 Monday

8 Tuesday

9 Wednesday

10 Thursday

11 Friday

12 Saturday

13 Sunday

The Weeping Angels appear as statues and can only move if no-one is looking at them

		S	M	T	W	T	F	S	S	M	T	W	T	F	S	S
	1	2	3	4	5	6	7	8	9	10	11	12	13	14	15	16	17	18	19	20
21	22	23	24	25	26	27	28	29	30

APRIL

The Doctor and Amy discover that everything
they are reading in a mystery book by
Melody Malone is becoming real

River Song, otherwise
known as Melody Malone,
writer of mystery books

THE ANGELS TAKE MANHATTAN

THE SNOWMEN

Devastated by the loss of Amy and Rory, the
Doctor retreats to a cloud in Victorian England.
There he meets a young woman called Clara,
and together they face the sinister Doctor
Simeon and an army of snowmen.

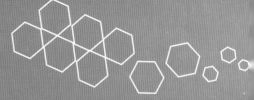

M	T	W	T	F	S	S	M	T	W	T	F	S	S	M	T	W	T	F	S	S
	1	2	3	4	5	6	7	8	9	10	11	12	13	14	15	16	17	18	19	20
21	22	23	24	25	26	27	28	29	30											

APRIL

14 **Monday**

Passover (begins at sundown)

15 **Tuesday**

16 **Wednesday**

17 **Thursday**

18 **Friday**

Good Friday

19 **Saturday**

20 **Sunday**

Easter Sunday

THE SNOWMEN (CHRISTMAS SPECIAL)

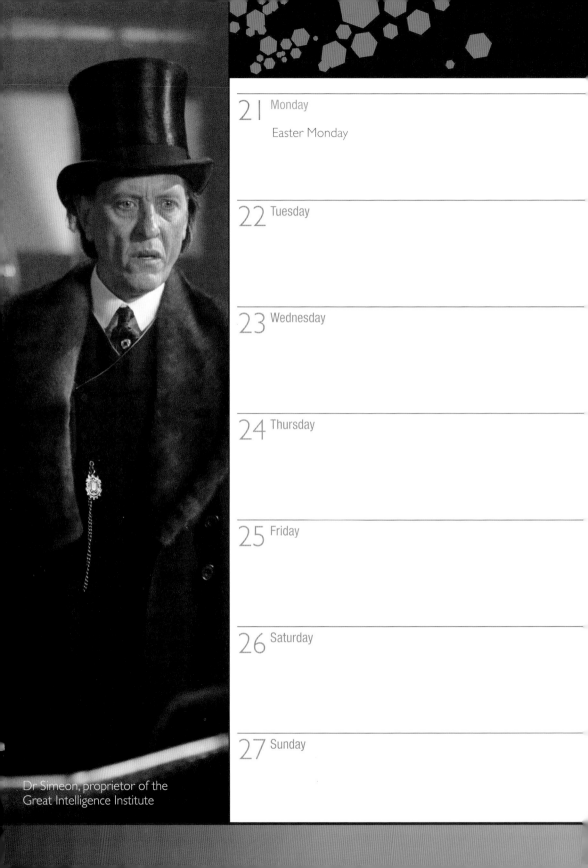

21 | Monday

Easter Monday

22 Tuesday

23 Wednesday

24 Thursday

25 Friday

26 Saturday

27 Sunday

Dr Simeon, proprietor of the
Great Intelligence Institute

M	T	W	T	F	S	S	M	T	W	T	F	S	S
1	2	3	4	5	6	7	8	9	10	11	12	13	14	15	16	17	18	19	20
21	22	23	24	25	26	27	28	29	30

APRIL

Clara, in the Victorian era,
works as a governess
and a barmaid

THE SNOWMEN (CHRISTMAS SPECIAL)

28 Monday

29 Tuesday

30 Wednesday

1 Thursday

MAY

2 Friday

3 Saturday

4 Sunday

The Doctor poses as Sherlock Holmes to gain entrance to the Great Intelligence Institute

M T W T F S S M T W T F S S M T W T F S S
1 2 3 4 5 6 7 8 9 10 11 12 13 14 15 16 17 18 19 20
21 22 23 24 25 26 27 28 29 30

APRIL

Silurian Madame Vastra, her wife
Jenny Flint and Sontaran Strax
help the Doctor uncover the
mystery of the Snowmen

The Snowmen
on the prowl

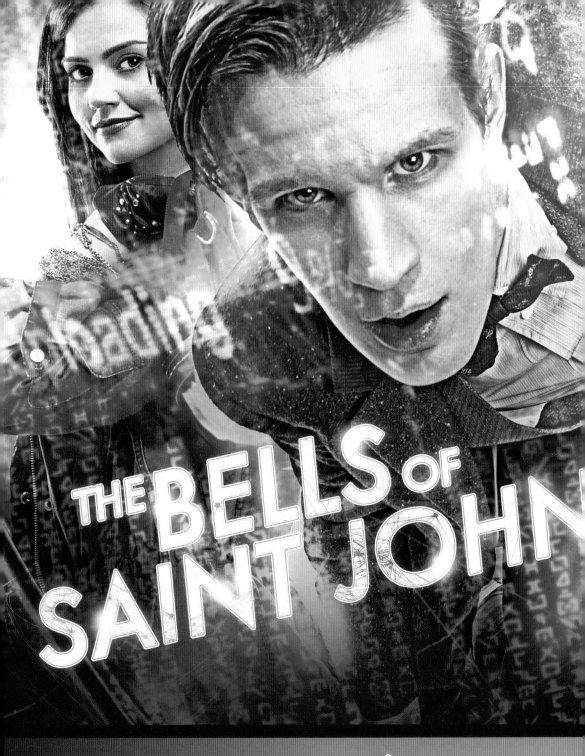

THE BELLS OF SAINT JOHN

The Doctor's search for Clara Oswald brings him to modern-day London where wi-fi is everywhere. But something dangerous is lurking in the signals, uploading people's souls and imprisoning them. When Clara becomes a victim the Doctor races to save her and the world from an ancient enemy.

M T W T F S S M T W T F S S M T W T F S S
1 2 3 4 5 6 7 8 9 10 11 12 13 14 15 16 17 18
19 20 21 22 23 24 25 26 27 28 29 30 31

MAY

5 **Monday**

6 **Tuesday**

7 **Wednesday**

8 **Thursday**

9 **Friday**

A character from a book
Clara is reading is used as
a disguise by a 'Spoonhead'
robotic mobile server

10 **Saturday**

11 **Sunday**

Mother's Day

12 Monday

13 Tuesday

14 Wednesday

15 Thursday

16 Friday

17 Saturday

18 Sunday

After his time of contemplation at the monastery the Doctor returns to modern-day London to find Clara

The Doctor painted this picture of
Clara to help him figure out the mystery
surrounding her

Miss Kizlet, head of the
computer organisation
that is uploading people

Don't click on this message, or you
will be uploaded!

TFOX =FΔTS

THE BELLS OF SAINT JOHN

Clara calls for assistance with her computer

19 Monday

20 Tuesday

21 Wednesday

22 Thursday

23 Friday

24 Saturday

25 Sunday

M	T	W	T	F	S	S	M	T	W	T	F	S	S
1	2	3	4	5	6	7	8	9	10	11	12	13	14	15	16	17	18
19	20	21	22	23	24	25	26	27	28	29	30	31

MAY

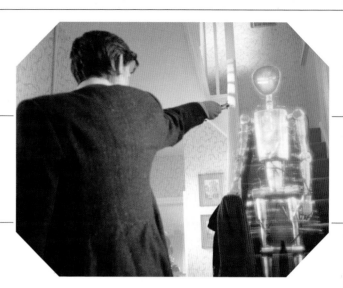

The Doctor confronts the 'Spoonhead' and
is able to save Clara from being uploaded

At a cafe with Clara, the Doctor
uses her laptop to try to work
out what is going on

| 26 | Monday |
| | Memorial Day |

| 27 | Tuesday |

| 28 | Wednesday |

| 29 | Thursday |

| 30 | Friday |

| 31 | Saturday |

| | Sunday |

JUNE

Clara takes her first bumpy
ride in the TARDIS

			M	T	W	T	F	S	S	S	M	T		F	S	S
		1	2	3	4	5	6	7	8	9	10	11	12	13	14	15	16	17	18
19	20	21	22	23	24	25	26	27	28	29	30	31				

MAY

Miss Kizlet and two employees
manage to upload and successfully
trap Clara before the Doctor
can intervene

The Doctor and Clara take an eventful ride
through London on an anti-gravity motorbike

THE BELLS OF SAINT JOHN

The Rings of Akhaten

The Doctor takes Clara on her first trip to an alien
world to see the wonders of the Rings of Akhaten.
There Clara meets young Merry, the Queen of Years.
She is to sing a special ceremonial lullaby at the Festival
of Offerings to keep the Old God asleep. But instead
he awakens, angry and demanding a sacrifice …

2 Monday

3 Tuesday

4 Wednesday

5 Thursday

6 Friday

7 Saturday

8 Sunday

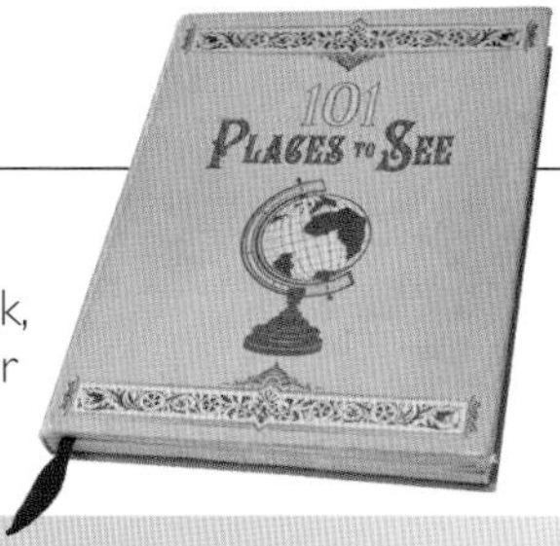

Clara's special book, given to her by her mother

THE RINGS OF AKHATEN

9 Monday

10 Tuesday

11 Wednesday

12 Thursday

13 Friday

14 Saturday

15 Sunday

Father's Day

The Doctor offers Clara a special type of fruit as they walk through a market on an asteroid in the Rings of Akhaten

					M	T	W	T	F	S	S	M	T	W	T	F	S	S
								1	2	3	4	5	6	7	8	9	10	11	12	13	14	15
16	17	18	19	20	21	22	23	24	25	26	27	28	29	30				

JUNE

The Doctor meets Clara and
her parents in his search to find
out who she is

Merry, the Queen of Years

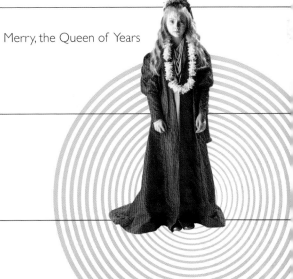

16 Monday

17 Tuesday

18 Wednesday

19 Thursday

20 Friday

21 Saturday

22 Sunday

The Old God, ,a planet-
sized parasitic creature,
awakens from his slumber
and he is not happy

			S	M	T	W	T	F	S	S	M	T	W			S	S
					1	2	3	4	5	6	7	8	9	10	11	12	13	14	15
16	17	18	19	20	21	22	23	24	25	26	27	28	29	30			

The Vigil, charged with looking after the Old God,
known as Grandfather

A mummy comes to life
and tries to attack Merry,
the Queen of Years

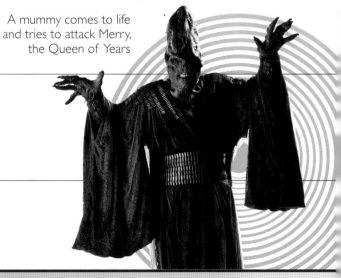

THE RINGS OF AKHATEN

Young Merry, the Queen of Years, begins to sing her special lullaby, 'The Long Song', to the Old God to keep him asleep

23 Monday

24 Tuesday

25 Wednesday

26 Thursday

27 Friday

28 Saturday

29 Sunday

M	T	W	T	F	S	S	M	T	W	T	F	S	S
				1	2	3	4	5	6	7	8	9	10	11	12	13	14	15
16	17	18	19	20	21	22	23	24	25	26	27	28	29	30

JUNE

Clara holds up the leaf her mother
kept from the day she first met
Clara's dad, as an offering to
the Old God

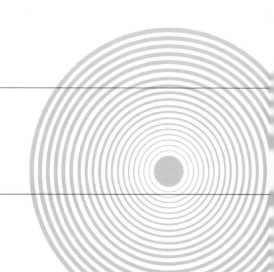

THE RINGS OF AKHATEN

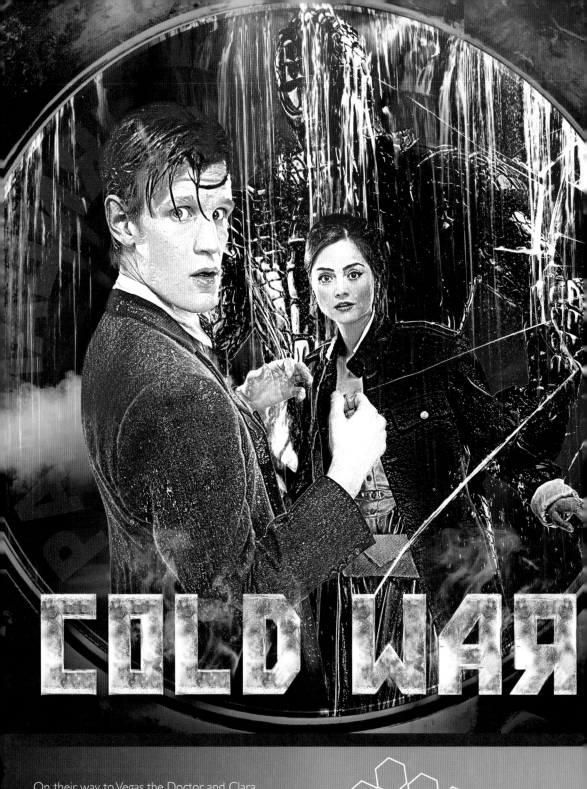

COLD WAR

On their way to Vegas the Doctor and Clara
materialise on a sinking Russian submarine in
1983. With oxygen supplies running low, they
must try to save the crew and themselves
before a bigger threat emerges – an Ice Warrior.

M	T	W	T	F	S	S	M	T	W	T	F	S	S	M	T	W	T	F	S	S
	1	2	3	4	5	6	7	8	9	10	11	12	13	14	15	16	17	18	19	20
21	22	23	24	25	26	27	28	29	30	31										

JULY

30 Monday

1 Tuesday

Canada Day

JULY

2 Wednesday

3 Thursday

4 Friday

Independence Day

5 Saturday

6 Sunday

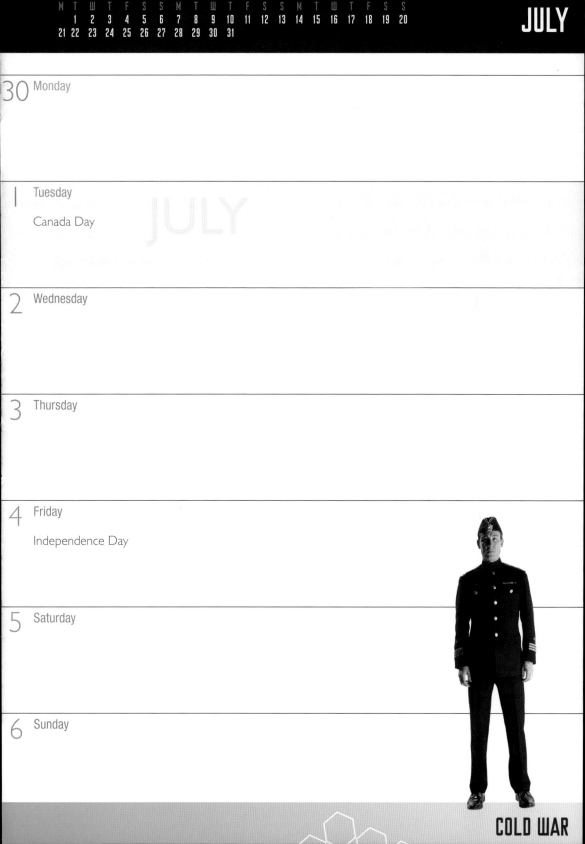

COLD WAR

7 Monday

8 Tuesday

9 Wednesday

10 Thursday

11 Friday

12 Saturday

13 Sunday

Clara lies unconscious after
the submarine crashes to
the ocean floor

The Doctor and Captain Zhukov discuss
how to approach Skaldak

Grand Marshall Skaldak is
an Ice Warrior who has
been stranded on Earth for
thousands of years

COLD WAR

14 Monday

15 Tuesday

16 Wednesday

17 Thursday

18 Friday

19 Saturday

20 Sunday

Against the Doctor's advice, the crew attack Skaldak and chain him up, making him very angry

										M	T	W	T	F	S	S	M	T	W	T	F	S	S
	1	2	3	4	5	6	7	8	9	10	11	12	13	14	15	16	17	18	19	20
21	22	23	24	25	26	27	28	29	30	31

The submarine is leaking water
as the Doctor tries to save both
the crew and Skaldak

COLD WAR

21 Monday

22 Tuesday

23 Wednesday

24 Thursday

25 Friday

26 Saturday

27 Sunday

The Ice Warrior
mothership
hovers over the
submarine to
retrieve their lost
warrior Skaldak

JULY

						S	S	M	T	W	T	F	S	S	M	T			F	S	S
1	2	3	4	5	6	7	8	9	10	11	12	13	14	15	16	17	18	19	20
21	22	23	24	25	26	27	28	29	30	31

Skaldak emerges from his armour
as his ship arrives for him

HIDE

The Doctor and Clara help out legendary ghost hunter Alec Palmer and his assistant, Emma, who are trying to contact a fabled spirit in a haunted house. Instead they discover a human time traveller caught in the Hex, a collapsing, imploding universe.

M T W T F S S S M T W T F S S S M T W T F S S
1 2 3 4 5 6 7 8 9 10 11 12 13 14 15 16 17
18 19 20 21 22 23 24 25 26 27 28 29 30 31

AUGUST

28 Monday

29 Tuesday

30 Wednesday

31 Thursday

| Friday

AUGUST

2 Saturday

Emma Grayling is
a psychic who has
found a connection
to a strange ghost

3 Sunday

HIDE

4 Monday

5 Tuesday

6 Wednesday

7 Thursday

8 Friday

9 Saturday

10 Sunday

Alec Palmer is
persuaded that the
Doctor is from the
Secret Service, so
allows him to assist
with the ghost hunt

M	T	W	T	F	S	S	M	T	W	T	F	S	S
			1	2	3	4	5	6	7	8	9	10	11	12	13	14	15	16	17
18	19	20	21	22	23	24	25	26	27	28	29	30	31

AUGUST

The Doctor gets very excited about the ghostly presence,
while Alec stands by to photograph any evidence

Emma Grayling, who
has strong psychic
powers, is sent to lure
the ghost out of hiding

11	Monday
12	Tuesday
13	Wednesday
14	Thursday
15	Friday
16	Saturday
17	Sunday

AUGUST

Alec and Emma have often caught
the ghost on film

The ghost is a time-travelling human
from the future, called Hila

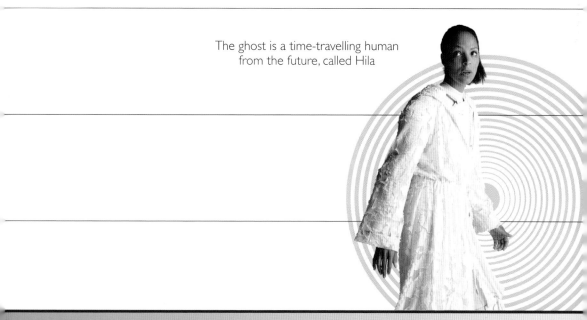

HIDE

18	Monday
19	Tuesday
20	Wednesday
21	Thursday
22	Friday
23	Saturday
24	Sunday

The Doctor travels in the
TARDIS from the beginning
until the end of time in
order to work out the
identity of the ghost

AUGUST

M	T	W	T	F	S	S	M	T	W	T	F	S	S
1	2	3	4	5	6	7	8	9	10	11	12	13	14	15	16	17
18	19	20	21	22	23	24	25	26	27	28	29	30	31

The Doctor runs through the Hex forest, trying to find
Hila and avoid the creature that is terrorising her

Clara pleads with the
TARDIS to help her
save the Doctor

25 Monday

26 Tuesday

27 Wednesday

28 Thursday

29 Friday

30 Saturday

31 Sunday

The menace follows the Doctor and Hila to the portal escape route

					M	T	W	T	F	S	S	S	M	T		F	S	S
			1	2	3	4	5	6	7	8	9	10	11	12	13	14	15	16	17
18	19	20	21	22	23	24	25	26	27	28	29	30	31					

AUGUST

Realising the creature was
just trying to find its mate, the
Doctor goes back into the Hex
to rescue the lovesick creature

HIDE

JOURNEY TO THE CENTRE OF THE TARDIS

Clara is lost in the depths of the TARDIS which is invaded by an intergalactic salvage crew who want to sell it for scrap, but the Doctor threatens to destroy the TARDIS by putting it in lock-down and activating the self destruct if the salvage crew doesn't help him find Clara.

SEPTEMBER

SEPTEMBER

1 Monday

Labor Day

2 Tuesday

3 Wednesday

4 Thursday

5 Friday

6 Saturday

7 Sunday

JOURNEY TO THE CENTRE OF THE TARDIS

The console is badly damaged after the TARDIS is roughly grabbed by the salvage ship's Magno-grab

8 Monday

9 Tuesday

10 Wednesday

11 Thursday

12 Friday

13 Saturday

14 Sunday

					S	M	T	W	T	F	S	S	M	T			F	S	S
1	2	3	4	5	6	7	8	9	10	11	12	13	14	15	16	17	18	19	20	21
22	23	24	25	26	27	28	29	30

SEPTEMBER

The Doctor meets a space salvage
crew and convinces them to help
him find Clara, who is lost
somewhere in the TARDIS

Gregor, one of the Van
Baalen brothers

15	Monday
16	Tuesday
17	Wednesday
18	Thursday
19	Friday
20	Saturday
21	Sunday

					S	M	T	W	T	F	S	S	M	T	W			F	S	S
1	2	3	4	5	6	7	8	9	10	11	12	13	14	15	16	17	18	19	20	21
22	23	24	25	26	27	28	29	30												

SEPTEMBER

The Van Baalen brothers realise the salvage
potential of the broken TARDIS and go in
search of good parts

The damaged TARDIS creates a labyrinth to protect itself, and Clara becomes lost in the maze

22 Monday

23 Tuesday

24 Wednesday

Rosh Hashanah (begins at sundown)

25 Thursday

26 Friday

27 Saturday

28 Sunday

S	S	M	T	W	T	F	S	S	M	T	W	T	F	S	S
1	2	3	4	5	6	7	8	9	10	11	12	13	14	15	16	17	18	19	20	21
22	23	24	25	26	27	28	29	30

SEPTEMBER

Clara finds herself in a huge library, where
she tries to stay hidden from a zombie-like
creature intent on finding her

The Doctor works out that a time
leak has occurred and realises that
he has to fix it to save the TARDIS
and all on board

THE CRIMSON HORROR

SWEETVILLE

In Victorian Yorkshire bodies are washing up in the river with glowing red skin. As they try to uncover the mystery, the Doctor and Clara are led to Sweetville, an idealised factory community on the surface with a sinister world-threatening danger lurking beneath…

M T W T F S S M T W T F S S M T W T F S S
1 2 3 4 5 6 7 8 9 10 11 12 13 14 15 16 17 18 19
20 21 22 23 24 25 26 27 28 29 30 31

OCTOBER

29 Monday

30 Tuesday

1 Wednesday

OCTOBER

2 Thursday

3 Friday

Yom Kippur (begins at sundown)

4 Saturday

5 Sunday

THE CRIMSON HORROR

6 Monday

7 Tuesday

8 Wednesday

9 Thursday

10 Friday

11 Saturday

12 Sunday

The Doctor and Clara
investigate the seemingly idyllic
community of Sweetville

S	M	T	W	T	F	S	S	M	T	W	T	F	S	S
	1	2	3	4	5	6	7	8	9	10	11	12	13	14	15	16	17	18	19

20 21 22 23 24 25 26 27 28 29 30 31

OCTOBER

Mrs Gillyflower plans to destroy everyone on the Earth,
except for her preserved 'perfect' people

Prehistoric red leech
'Mr Sweet' who had a
symbiotic relationship
with Mrs Gillyflower

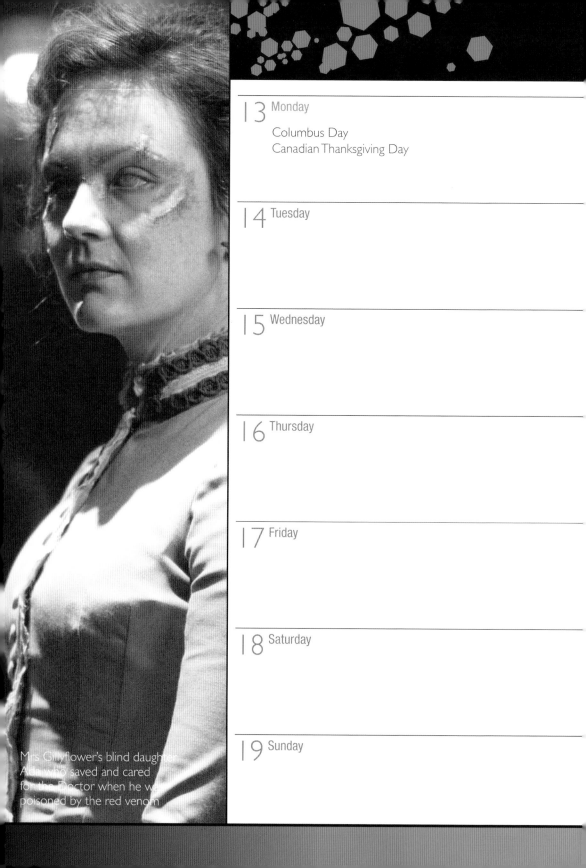

13 Monday

Columbus Day
Canadian Thanksgiving Day

14 Tuesday

15 Wednesday

16 Thursday

17 Friday

18 Saturday

19 Sunday

Mrs Gillyflower's blind daughter
Ada who saved and cared
for the Doctor when he was
poisoned by the red venom

M T W T F S S M T W T F S S M T W T F S S
1 2 3 4 5 6 7 8 9 10 11 12 13 14 15 16 17 18 19
20 21 22 23 24 25 26 27 28 29 30 31

OCTOBER

Jenny investigates the factory to find it empty apart from
horns blasting out recorded industrial noise

THE CRIMSON HORROR

The poisoned Doctor is unable to walk or talk properly

20 Monday

21 Tuesday

22 Wednesday

23 Thursday

24 Friday

25 Saturday

26 Sunday

	M	T	W	T	F	S	S	M	T	W	T	F	S	S	M	T	W	T	F	S	S
			1	2	3	4	5	6	7	8	9	10	11	12	13	14	15	16	17	18	19
20	21	22	23	24	25	26	27	28	29	30	31

OCTOBER

The Doctor, Clara, Jenny and Madame Vastra race to stop
Mrs Gillyflower from poisoning the world

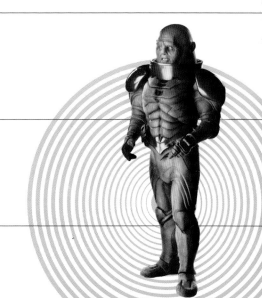

27 Monday

28 Tuesday

29 Wednesday

30 Thursday

31 Friday

Halloween

| Saturday

NOVEMBE

2 Sunday

Daylight Saving (end)

Clara is successfully
placed in one of
Sweetvilles' preservation
domes

The many factories of the industrial North
allowed Mrs Gillyflower to use Sweetville
as a cover for her evil plans

Sweetville wasn't the perfect
community it pretended to be
and hid a terrifying secret

NIGHTMARE IN SILVER

The Doctor and Clara travel to Hedgewick's World of Wonders – a planet-sized theme park. But Cybermen have taken over, including the Cyber-Planner who challenges the Doctor to a game of chess with terrifying stakes…

M T W T F S S M T W T F S S M T W T F S S
1 2 3 4 5 6 7 8 9 10 11 12 13 14 15 16
17 18 19 20 21 22 23 24 25 26 27 28 29 30

NOVEMBER

3 Monday

4 Tuesday

5 Wednesday

6 Thursday

7 Friday

8 Saturday

9 Sunday

NIGHTMARE IN SILVER

10 Monday

11 Tuesday

Veterans' Day

12 Wednesday

13 Thursday

14 Friday

15 Saturday

16 Sunday

The Doctor and
Clara take Artie and
Angie to the greatest
theme park in the
galaxy

M	T	W	T	F	S	S	M	T	W	T		F	S	S
	1	2	3	4	5	6	7	8	9	10	11	12	13	14	15	16
17	18	19	20	21	22	23	24	25	26	27	28	29	30			

NOVEMBER

Although it looks like the surface of the moon,
this is a ride called the 'Spacey Zoomer'

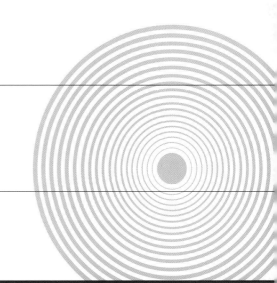

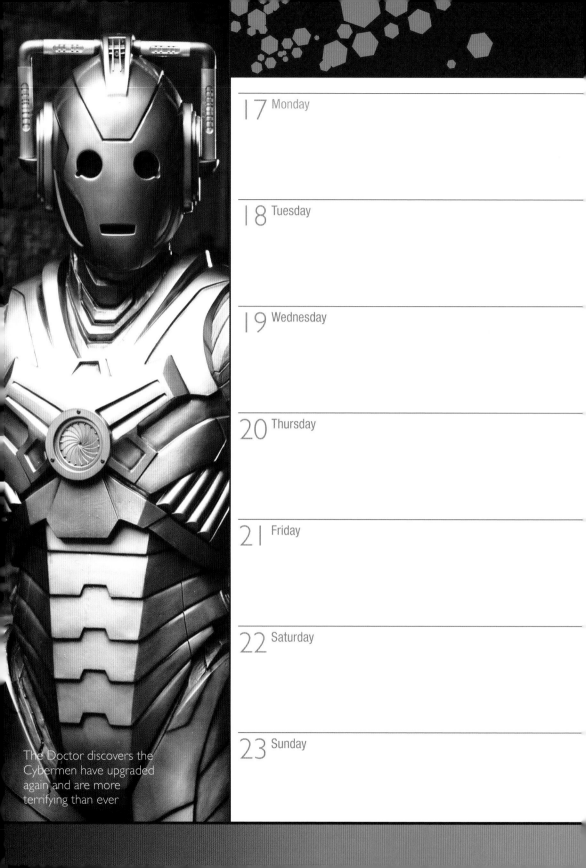

17 Monday

18 Tuesday

19 Wednesday

20 Thursday

21 Friday

22 Saturday

23 Sunday

The Doctor discovers the
Cybermen have upgraded
again and are more
terrifying than ever

			S	M	T	W	T	F	S	S	M	T			F	S	S	
					1	2	3	4	5	6	7	8	9	10	11	12	13	14	15	16
17	18	19	20	21	22	23	24	25	26	27	28	29	30					

NOVEMBER

Clara and a group of soldiers try
to hold off the Cyber army

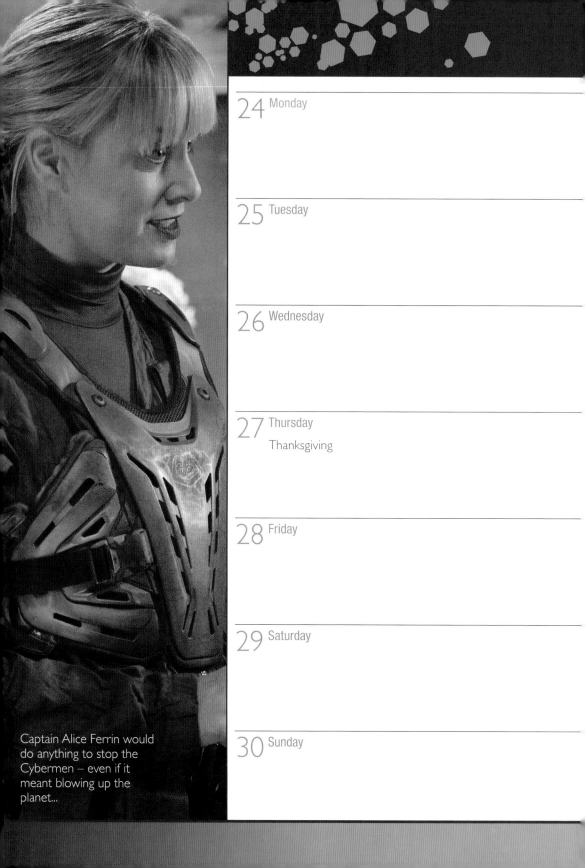

24 Monday

25 Tuesday

26 Wednesday

27 Thursday
Thanksgiving

28 Friday

29 Saturday

30 Sunday

Captain Alice Ferrin would do anything to stop the Cybermen – even if it meant blowing up the planet...

			S	M	T	W	T	F	S	S	M	T	W	T	F	S	S
					1	2	3	4	5	6	7	8	9	10	11	12	13	14	15	16
17	18	19	20	21	22	23	24	25	26	27	28	29	30

NOVEMBER

The Doctor tries to fend off an incredibly fast
Cyberman who kidnaps Angie

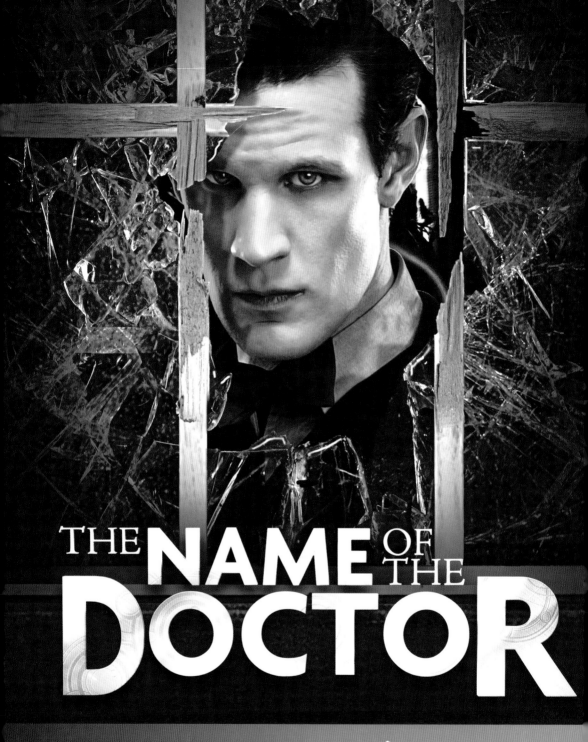

THE NAME OF THE DOCTOR

After his friends are kidnapped by the Great
Intelligence, the Doctor and Clara travel to the one
place he should never go – the planet Trenzalore
where his tomb is located, along with a deadly trap...

M T W T F S S M T W T F S S M T W T F S S
1 2 3 4 5 6 7 8 9 10 11 12 13 14 15 16 17 18 19 20 21
22 23 24 25 26 27 28 29 30 31

DECEMBER

1	Monday

DECEMBER

2	Tuesday

3	Wednesday

4	Thursday

5	Friday

6	Saturday

7	Sunday

THE NAME OF THE DOCTOR

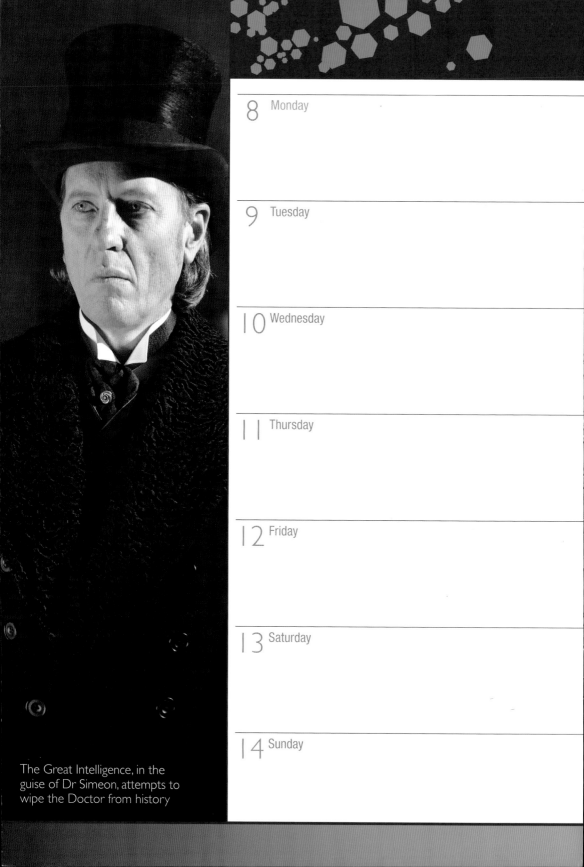

8	Monday
9	Tuesday
10	Wednesday
11	Thursday
12	Friday
13	Saturday
14	Sunday

The Great Intelligence, in the guise of Dr Simeon, attempts to wipe the Doctor from history

| 1 | 2 | 3 | 4 | 5 | 6 | 7 | 8 | 9 | 10 | 11 | 12 | 13 | 14 | 15 | 16 | 17 | 18 | 19 | 20 | 21 |
| 22 | 23 | 24 | 25 | 26 | 27 | 28 | 29 | 30 | 31 |

The deadly Whisper Men are the servants
of the Great Intelligence

Madame Vastra holds a
'conference call' in a dreamscape
of her own making with River,
Clara, Jenny and Strax

THE NAME OF THE DOCTOR

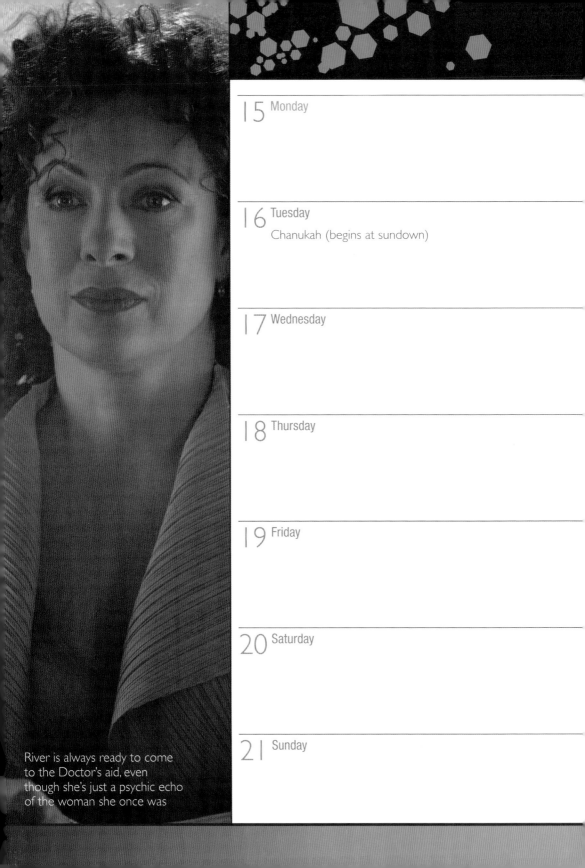

15 Monday

16 Tuesday
Chanukah (begins at sundown)

17 Wednesday

18 Thursday

19 Friday

20 Saturday

21 Sunday

River is always ready to come to the Doctor's aid, even though she's just a psychic echo of the woman she once was

1	2	3	4	5	6	7	8	9	10	11	12	13	14	15	16	17	18	19	20	21
22	23	24	25	26	27	28	29	30	31											

The Whisper Men capture Madame Vastra, Jenny and Strax to lure the Doctor to Trenzalore

Strax reverts to his true Sontaran ways when the Doctor vanishes from the timeline

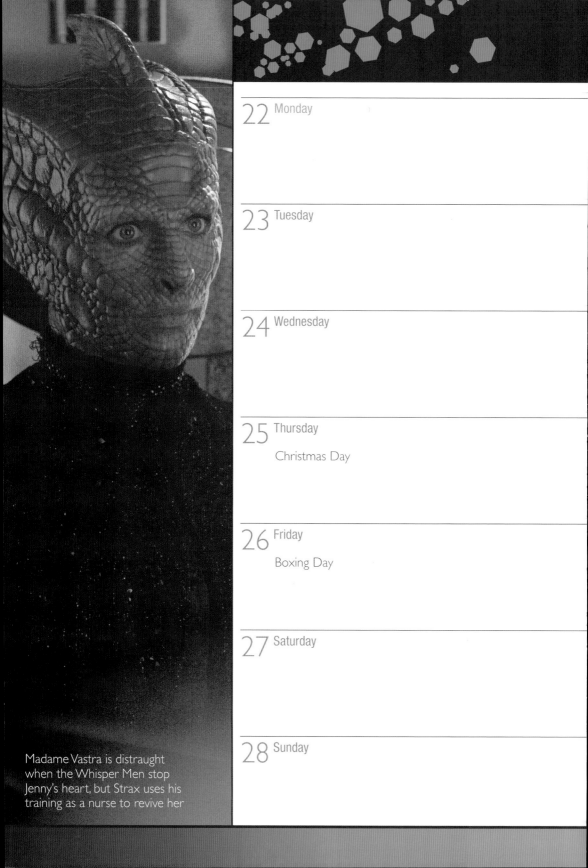

22 Monday

23 Tuesday

24 Wednesday

25 Thursday

Christmas Day

26 Friday

Boxing Day

27 Saturday

28 Sunday

Madame Vastra is distraught
when the Whisper Men stop
Jenny's heart, but Strax uses his
training as a nurse to revive her

DECEMBER

M	T	W	T	F	S	S	M	T	W	T	F	S	S
1	2	3	4	5	6	7	8	9	10	11	12	13	14	15	16	17	18	19	20	21
22	23	24	25	26	27	28	29	30	31

The Great Intelligence can transfer himself between Whisper Men, transforming his appearance to look like Doctor Simeon

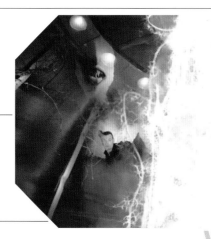

The Great Intelligence tries to infect the Doctor's entire timeline through the time stream nexus in the centre of the TARDIS tomb

29 Monday

30 Tuesday

31 Wednesday

New Year's Eve

1 Thursday

New Year's Day

JANUARY

2 Friday

3 Saturday

4 Sunday

The Whisper Men have the power to stop people's hearts and they threaten to kill his friends if the Doctor doesn't do as the Great Intelligence asks

M	T	W	T	F	S	S	M	T	W	T	F	S	S	M	T	W	T	F	S	S
1	2	3	4	5	6	7	8	9	10	11	12	13	14	15	16	17	18	19	20	21
22	23	24	25	26	27	28	29	30	31											

DECEMBER

Even when threatened the Doctor stands up to the evil entity he has beaten many times before

Clara comforts the convulsing Doctor as his past begins to be erased

Published in 2013 by Mallon Publishing Pty Limited

PO Box 1210 Research Victoria Australia 3095

Produced by Mallon Publishing Pty Limited
Designer Bec Yule @ Red Chilli Design
Editor Margaret Trudgeon
Compilation and design © 2013 Mallon Publishing Pty Limited

Printed in China through Asia Pacific Offset Ltd

Distributed in the USA by Diamond Comic Distributors Inc.
10150 York Road Suite 300 Hunt Valley, Maryland 21030